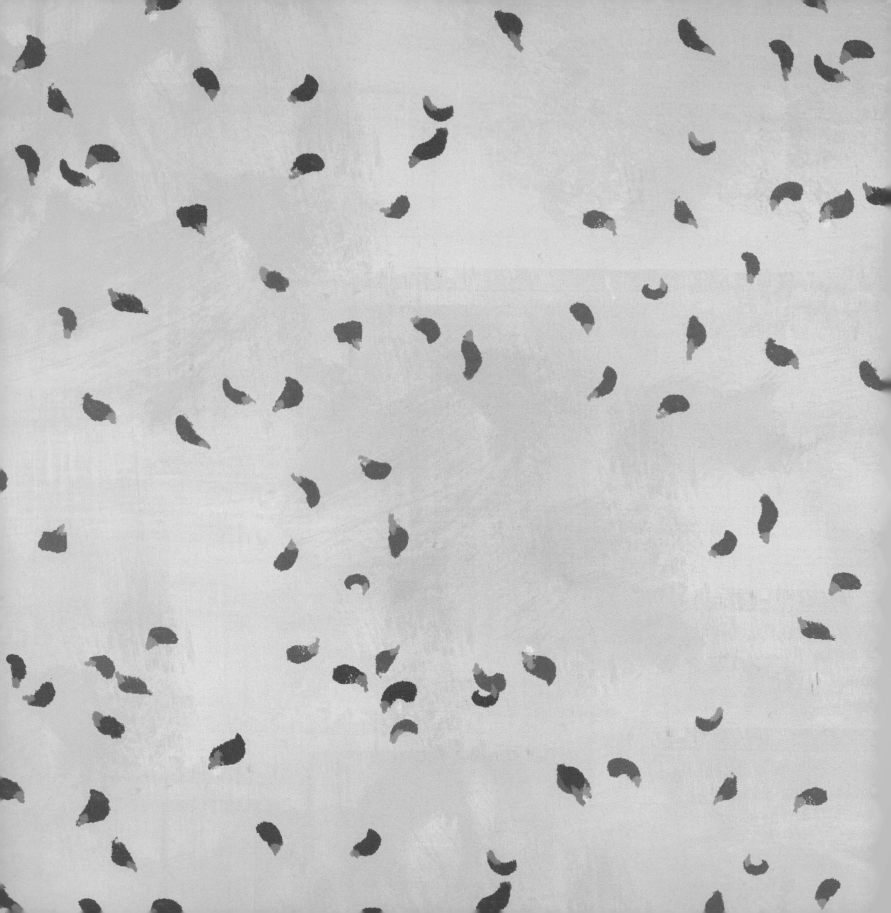

FLOWER GIRL

FLOWER GIRL

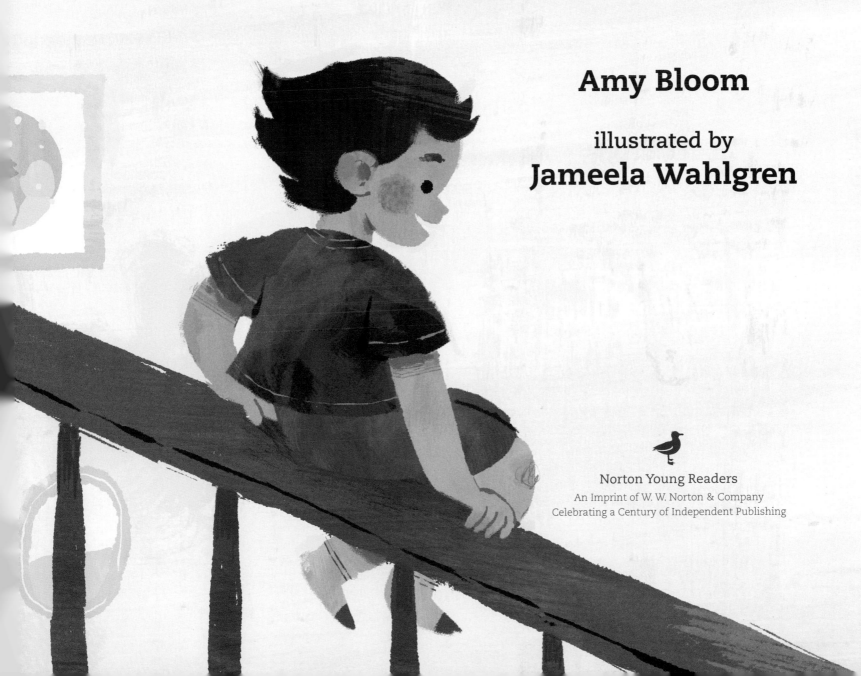

Amy Bloom

illustrated by
Jameela Wahlgren

Norton Young Readers
An Imprint of W. W. Norton & Company
Celebrating a Century of Independent Publishing

For the Fab Four

Zora
Ivy
Eden
Izzy

—A.B.

For my agent, Hannah, who believed in me.

—J.W.

For information about permission to reproduce selections from this book, write to
Permissions, W. W. Norton & Company, Inc., 500 Fifth Avenue, New York, NY 10110

For information about special discounts for bulk purchases, please contact W. W. Norton
Special Sales at specialsales@wwnorton.com or 800-233-4830

Manufacturing by Toppan Leefung
Book design by Hana Anouk Nakamura
Production managers: Anna Oler & Delaney Adams

ISBN 978-1-324-03035-5

W. W. Norton & Company, Inc., 500 Fifth Avenue, New York, N.Y. 10110
www.wwnorton.com

W. W. Norton & Company Ltd., 15 Carlisle Street, London W1D 3BS

1 2 3 4 5 6 7 8 9 0

Nicki came downstairs one morning
and checked out the world.

Sun shining. Clouds fluffy. Pancakes cooking.
A perfect morning.

And then . . . it got better!

Aunt Carmela came over.
Aunt Carmela was the best aunt.
The funnest aunt.
The coolest aunt.

Everyone ate Dad's Super Blueberry Pancakes and Aunt Carmela
told them that she was getting married—to Big Dave.

Nicki loved Big Dave. He was nice, and funny, and really, very, very useful.

When they got married, he'd be Uncle Big Dave—and that was great news.

And then . . . it got better!

Aunt Carmela asked Nicki: Will you be our Flower Girl?

Would she? Would she?

You bet she would.

"Just one thing," said Nicki. "What's a Flower Girl?"

Aunt Carmela said, "A Flower Girl is the first person, just about the most important person, of the wedding. The Flower Girl spreads flower petals before anyone else walks into the room."

"Why?" Nicki asked.

"Because it's pretty," Dad said.

"And it's a sign of love," Mama said.

"Okay," said Nicki. "I am all in for love and pretty petals!"

And all day long, that's what she thought about.

Aunt Carmela called the next day and said, "Let's go, Tiger."

Nicki loved when Aunt Carmela called her Tiger.

"We're off on an adventure," Mama said.

"There will be ice cream," Aunt Carmela said.

The first stop was the wedding dress store.

Aunt Carmela looked beautiful.

"Yay," said Nicki. "You are GORGEOUS!"

Aunt Carmela hugged Nicki hard.

Then she showed Nicki a small dress.

"How about this one?" Mama said.

"For who?" Nicki said.

"For you," Aunt Carmela and Mama both said.

Nicki said nothing.

After a while, Mama said, "Let's get that ice cream."

When they got home, Aunt Carmela said, "Let's try again."

She got out a big magazine with lots of pictures. There sure were a lot of little dresses!

Nicki said nothing.

After a while, Nicki said, very politely, "Thank you for the ice cream." And she went to her room.

Aunt Carmela knocked on Nicki's door.

"Tiger, I have to go. Don't worry, we'll find a dress you like."

Nicki said nothing.

Aunt Carmela said, "You'll be a beautiful Flower Girl."

Nicki said very, very quietly, "I don't want to be a Flower Girl."

Aunt Carmela was surprised. She told Mama, and Mama was surprised.

Nicki sat through dinner and she sat through playtime and she didn't say another word.

The next morning, Nicki came downstairs and checked out the day.

Dad made his Super Blueberry Pancakes but . . .

Dad asked, "Is it true you don't want to be a Flower Girl?"

Nicki nodded.

"Are you still all in for love and pretty petals?"

Nicki nodded.

She went back to her room to think things over.

Nicki said, "I'm not really a dress kind of girl."

Dad nodded. "Never have been."

"Let's go shopping," Dad said. "There will be ice cream."

They were off on an adventure.

Dad tried on his suit.

"Yay," said Nicki. "You look GORGEOUS!"

"Now it's your turn," said Dad.

Nicki was a little nervous.

And then she was not!

"You're GORGEOUS!" Dad said.

"I guess I am," said Nicki.

On the wedding day, the sun was shining.
The clouds were fluffing and the pancakes were blueberry.

It was perfect.

And the wedding was just about perfect.

And then . . . it got better.

Aunt Carmela said, "Tiger, you gotta be you.
And YOU are the best Flower Girl ever."

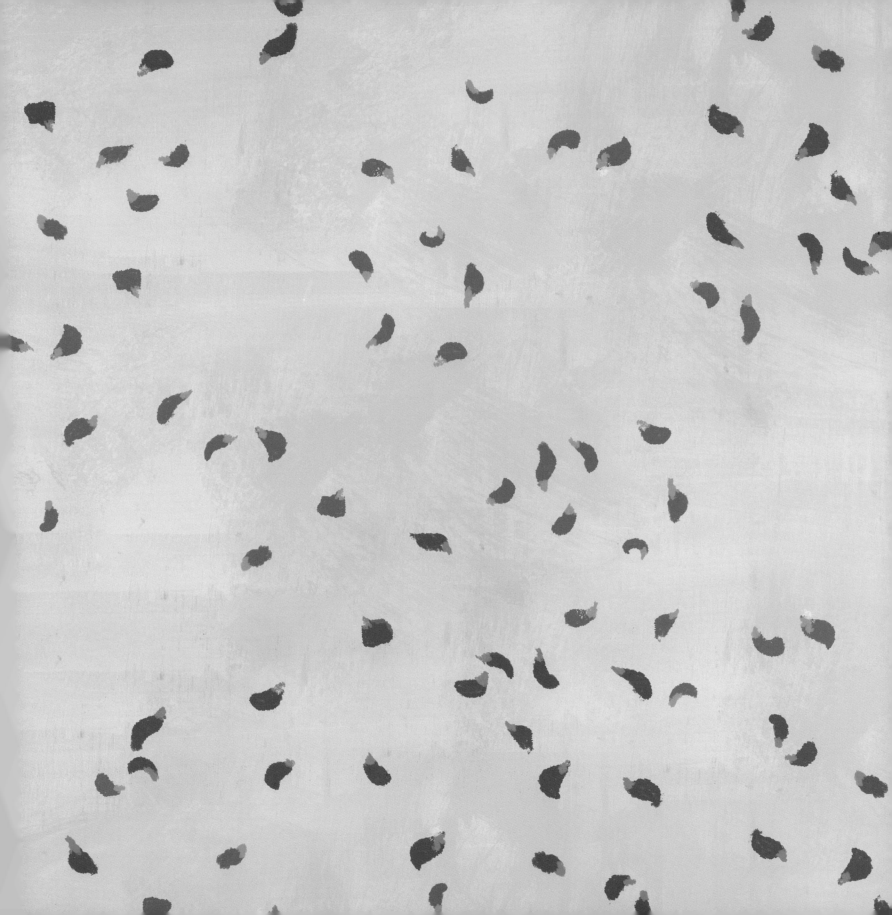

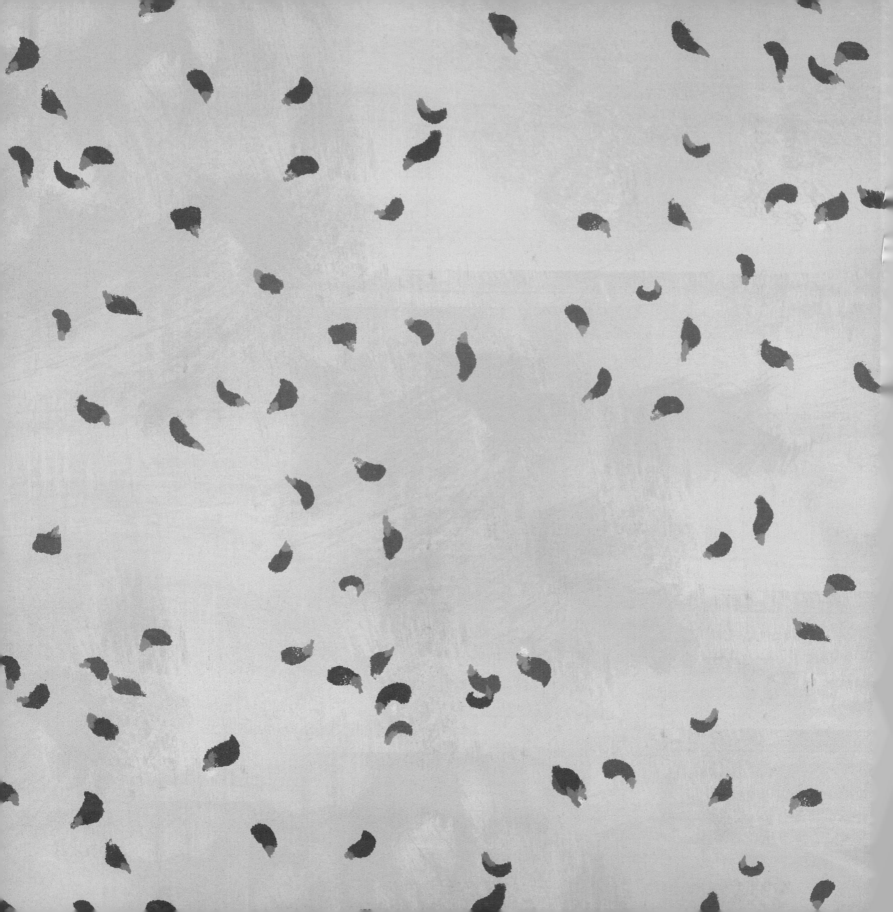